I0688982

WAR OF THE TWIN SWORDS

GEMSTONE MASSACRE SERIES PREQUEL

JULIA GOLDHIRSH

Copyright © 2020 by Julia Goldhirsh

All rights reserved.

No part of this book may be reproduced in any form or by any electronic or mechanical means, including information storage and retrieval systems, without written permission from the author, except for the use of brief quotations in a book review.

To my late grandmother, Rita. You'll always be my trailblazer and inspiration.

CHAPTER ONE

On the night before Argentum's Choosing ceremony, there were whispers of war in the air. The sorceresses had threatened to take Excalibur from their clan by force. Her mother's words kept cycling through Argentum's mind. *You'll need a strong gem to lead our clan,* her mother had said, lifting Argentum's chin with a manicured fingernail.

Argentum sighed. The tightness in her chest wouldn't ease, and sleep was out of reach. With a huff, she rolled out of bed and paced across the plush carpet of her bedroom floor, agonizing over what she'd do if she didn't receive a strong enough gemstone. She couldn't disappoint her parents. She would succeed them as the Enchantress Clan's leader the next day whether she liked it or not, but she would need a strong gem to stay in power. If she was too weak, another enchantress or enchanter would dethrone her.

But gemstone affinities aren't a choice. What am I supposed to do? She grabbed a pillow off the bed and threw it at the green plaster wall in frustration. It made her feel better, but she still didn't have answers.

Maybe the library did. She rubbed her eyes and slid on her

favorite fuzzy black slippers before shuffling to her parents' library to do some research. Even though it was just down the hall, the walk felt like an eternity. Her limbs were heavy with exhaustion, but her mind still raced.

She took a deep breath as she entered the rows upon rows of floor-to-ceiling shelves. The musty scent of freshly bound books and the hint of lemon cleaner lingering on the bookshelves and tables soothed her nerves. She ran her hands over one of the smooth oak bookshelves, searching for anything that seemed relevant.

Hours later, she was no closer to finding a way to influence the ceremony. The books all agreed; only a gemstone could choose its owner. She shoved the stack of books aside. This was useless.

As she finished putting the books away, a ragged book covered with dust caught her attention. She blew on its cover to remove the thick layer of dust coating its surface, revealing "Opal" in a stunning silver script. Curiosity made her open the book.

There is a cavern near the portal that few enchantresses dare enter. It holds the strongest gemstone of them all, the Fire Opal. This is a gem that you can choose, but enchantresses beware...

The rest of the text had been ripped out. She ignored the pang of dread in her stomach and closed the book. *Whatever the danger, it's worth the risk to protect my clan. Without a powerful leader, one of the enemy clans will invade and kill us in droves.*

Argentum placed the book back on the shelf with the other Choosing books. She bounced her leg with excitement. She definitely wouldn't sleep knowing that she'd found a loophole— a way to get a powerful gem without having to rely on genetics or luck. The heel of her slippers scraped against the marble floors on the way to her room.

As soon as she was back in her room, surrounded by the comfort of her ivy-green walls and hardwood floors, her shoulders relaxed. She inhaled the calming scent of vanilla wafting from the oil infuser on her nightstand.

She grabbed a silver device imported from the human world and turned on some music to help her fall asleep. She closed her eyes, begging her mind to rest. It wasn't until the gray dawn peeked through the clouds that she drifted off to sleep.

~

Her mother flung open Argentum's blackout curtains, flooding the room with light.

"Five more minutes," Argentum said, pulling the covers over her face.

"No. We'll have none of that today. Get ready, and wear something regal. After your Choosing, you'll be the clan's new leader."

Argentum groaned as her mother snatched the covers and tossed them to the floor. Argentum pushed herself out of bed as her mother rustled through the closet.

"Goodness, Argentum, do you own any dresses?"

Argentum grabbed the brush from her dresser and brushed her hair quickly. "Can I just wear nice pants and a shirt today?" As much as her mom loved dresses, Argentum preferred the practicality of pants. No worries about how she sat, no material brushing over her legs at the slightest breeze...

Her mother let out a sigh. "Fine, just make sure they're nice."

Argentum smiled and kissed her mother on the cheek. "Now, get out so I can get dressed," Argentum teased, playfully pushing her mom toward the door.

She laughed. "Okay, okay. I'm going." She held up her hands in surrender as she exited the room.

Argentum tugged on her nicest black slacks and a belt with space for a sword and sheath, just in case. She slid on a pair of closed-toe black dress shoes—a compromise between the heels her mother wanted and the sneakers that called Argentum's name from the closet. For the final piece, she grabbed a silky V-neck blouse with short sleeves that shone with the same rainbow luster of an opal. Fitting for that day. *Beautiful and formal, but still easy to move in,* she thought as she admired herself in a full-length mirror. *A nice outfit for my eighteenth birthday and my Choosing.*

Today, she would get her true name, her enchantress name. Today, the fate of her clan would be placed in her hands.

She was the only person in the entire clan turning eighteen, so she would undertake her Choosing alone. Not that many people could say they were born on Halloween.

When she opened her bedroom door, she found her mother anxiously pacing back and forth in the hallway. "Well, at least you didn't wear all black this time," she said.

Argentum's father joined them; his lips curled up in a rare smile. "Good luck today." He moved closer and tucked a stray hair behind her ear. She gave a weak smile back, but nausea settled in her stomach.

Argentum pulled open the heavy mahogany entry doors and exited the mansion. The humid, salty air frizzed her hair, and she regretted not putting any hair products in it as they walked toward the entrance to Gemstone Forest.

Her body thrummed with nervous energy as they passed through the town. The majority of houses in this area of town were beige, white, and powder-blue houses with stark white wrap-around porches. A few rebels had older stucco houses, with the rare 1970s era split-level condos and a couple old restored castles from Merlin's era scattered throughout.

Off in the distance, she spotted the most rebellious house of all: a bubble-gum pink hut that the village elder, Coral, owned. Argentum could see the old woman watching from her front lawn but was too far away to tell if she smiled or scowled.

People gaped at Argentum and her parents as they walked

along, and while she recognized some of the crowd, it wasn't often that she mingled with the lower-ranked mages. After being teased relentlessly in elementary and middle school for her silver-white hair, she'd been switched over to private tutors. The attention made Argentum's nerves squirm.

When they reached the forest, her father, Tanzanite, leaned close to her ear and whispered. "Don't disappoint us."

She shivered despite the blazing sun. The forest was always colder than the rest of the village. Shaking her head and placing a hand on the trunk of a golden citrine tree, she took a few deep breaths to clear her head. Tension left her body as she inhaled the tree's honeyed scent.

I'll be fine. I have a plan. When she looked up, she glimpsed sapphire familiars, birds, swooping through the sky. She gazed in awe at the mesmerizing blue glimmer for a few seconds, but then she refocused on the task at hand—finding the Fire Opal familiar. She would need to move fast.

Usually, the gems picked you, but the cave she sought held the Fire Opal from the book—a gem she could choose. She wanted it despite the warning. *I guess I just can't resist playing with fire.*

As she ventured deeper into the forest, the creatures' appearances grew stranger. There was a jade beast that glowed with green magic trampling the crystalline grass of the forest floor as it trotted along. Its skin was marbled and swirled like a Van Gogh painting, but the creature resembled a stegosaurus, with spikes running along its humped spine. Black-and-white snow leopards made of snowflake obsidian yowled and scattered when she approached. Brown-and-gold tourmaline owls with ruby eyes hooted from their place in the treetops. She tasted hints of salt as she rushed past a placid tidal pool, cloudy-white selenite snakes hissing a warning as she passed by the water's edge.

She'd been walking for hours when she finally spotted it. A cavern glowing with a rainbow of red magic.

The mouth of the cave was encrusted with crimson rubies, fuchsia beryl, orange carnelians, and so many others crowded together like fans in a stadium. It vibrated with the magic of dormant gemstone creatures.

She ventured into the shimmering magic cavern. Its walls were lined with the gold and silver ore her clan used to forge necklaces and bracelets embedded with gems for protection. Beautiful, burning coral and bright fire-red agate littered the cave floor, but none of them took the form of a familiar.

Argentum prowled all over the cavern, but no familiars approached her. The sun's light grew dimmer as she continued to search the cave. Her throat closed as panic gripped her. The gems all stayed in hibernation, mocking her with their brilliant glow. *What if the Fire Opal was just a myth after all? What if no gems choose me?*

After a few more hours of walking through the cavern and wading through puddles of icy water that dampened her pant legs, she reached a dead end. A wall of rocks blocked her from going any farther. Still no luck.

Resigned to failure, she felt around the rough, gem-encrusted walls and headed back to the mouth of the cave. When she emerged and saw the orange rays of the setting sun, she wondered whether she would receive a familiar at all.

Argentum stole one last look at the cave. The portal to the human world writhed beside it. She turned away to head back to the village, but a sudden gust of wind knocked her off her feet.

She scrambled to regain her balance and dusted off her black pants. When she moved to get up, hot breath that smelled of brimstone brushed her face. She raised her head to see a creature she'd only dreamed of—a Fire Opal dragon. The familiar's wings shone with all the colors of a brilliant rainbow in the fading sun, and she could see fire settled in its transparent red-and-purple belly. Argentum rubbed her eyes to make sure she wasn't dreaming. She almost couldn't believe she was actually looking at a Fire Opal dragon.

It knelt before her. The dragon's strong voice echoed in her mind. *I pledge my allegiance to you. I will be your sword and shield and will protect you through any battle.*

Her jaw dropped. She fumbled for words, any words, until she remembered the next steps to seal the contract with her familiar.

She touched its lowered forehead with her palm and reached out with her own thoughts. *I accept your allegiance.*

At that, the dragon familiar changed shape. It expanded into a frenzied sphere of violet-and-crimson energy. When it had settled, she saw its other form: a sword embedded with a blood-red and dark-violet stone. It shone with a core that resembled a captured flame.

With a smile, she grabbed the sword and its sheath from the ground and fastened them both to the belt on her waist before heading back to town. With such a powerful familiar, she was no longer Argentum. She was Opal, and she was strong enough to lead her people.

CHAPTER TWO

When she reached the threshold of the forest, sunset had just turned to dusk.

It wasn't until she reached the village that her pride began to fade. The smiles of the awaiting townspeople disappeared as they caught a glimpse of the red glow emanating from her sheath. They backed away, faces scrunched in distaste. Even her own parents shrank away from the glow, jerking back instinctively when they saw her.

Her mother fought the reflexive reaction, but the sword still clearly pained her. She scrunched her eyes when she looked at the sword, as though trying to stare at the sun. Opal opened her mouth to inquire about what was happening, but her mother mouthed, "Later."

Opal's gaze darted around, taking in the villagers' panicked stares. Her mouth opened and closed like a fish out of water. *What did I do wrong? Why are they behaving this way?* Tears welled in her eyes. She reached for her mother, but her mother pulled away.

Coral, the village elder, stepped forward, her eyes rolling back until only the whites showed. In an otherworldly voice, she boomed, "A horrible omen of war. The first Fire Opal in centuries. All who touch its flames will be burned up in battle."

Opal's eyes widened. Her face flushed red in shame. *You tricked me!*

The sword's dark laughter echoed in her thoughts. *Ah, but it was you that sought me out, was it not?*

Her mother handed over the sign of her leadership, an enchanted ruby pin, to Opal. Her mother avoided eye contact with Opal throughout the entire ceremony. Opal had often pictured her rise to power, but this wasn't how she had wanted her rule to begin.

Her father shook his head. His eyes were full of disappointment. "What have you done?"

Opal began to regret her choice. What was power if the people she cared about cast her out? She could feel the rumbling of the dragon through the sword where the sheath touched her hip. It was too much, and tears stung her eyes. She'd prove them all wrong. The rest of the ceremony would have to wait.

Opal rushed past her mother, heading in the direction of home. Opal couldn't care less that she was cutting her leadership ceremony short. Her mother tried to grab Opal's hand, but she pulled away and took off running, and she didn't stop until she reached the front entrance. She could still feel her father's look of disappointment boring into her retreating back.

She searched her room for her bow, throwing the sheets to the floor in frustration and searching the gap between the bed and the wall. *Where is it?* She rummaged through her dresser. "Ugh. Where did Mother put it?" she muttered to herself as she frantically threw hair clips and loose gems from her nightstand to the floor.

Opal took a deep breath to calm herself and glanced at the metal hooks on the wall. Her bow and a full quiver of arrows were hanging up, waiting for her. "Of course, it's the last place I think to look. Mom moved it again."

She grabbed her bow and arrows before racing out into the dark forest separating the Enchantress Clan from the Sorceress Clan, her haven.

When she was deep into the thicket of trees, she looked up to gaze at the stars. Their blazing violet and sterling tones made her feel at ease. The forest winds whistled as if in approval of her arrival, and Opal removed her cloak so she could feel the cool night breeze caress her skin. She loved surrounding herself with the lush, sage-green trees. The trunks were thicker than three of her. They were perfect for archery practice.

Her eyes bored into one of the trees. She grabbed a quartz-infused arrow from her quiver and took the stance she'd been practicing since she could walk, feet squared and bow close to her chest. She grabbed and notched the enchanted arrow, breathing deeply to steady her mind, making sure her hand didn't waver as she aimed. Her index and middle fingers surrounded the arrow but didn't touch it, and she drew it back, tilting the bow slightly to the left as she aimed. The arrow filled with fire magic, her specialty.

As she breathed out, she channeled her pent-up rage into the point of the arrow, feeling warmth spread through her hand as she touched it. The sword vibrated with a deep roar of approval. Her mind finally felt calm.

She let the arrow fly.

It embedded itself in the middle of the tree's trunk before erupting into vivid white flames. The flames licked the tree but didn't spread. Then, the second part of her enchantment hit, and she backed up as the arrow exploded, scattering shards of crystal.

Assessing the damage, she was shocked to find a large hole the size of her body. *So, this is the power that comes with a Choosing.* Pride swelled within her. Finally, she was powerful.

The rustle of branches in a nearby treetop startled her. Someone was here. She grabbed another arrow and notched it, aiming her bow at the source of the noise, but she couldn't see her target. Fear coiled within her.

She'd come here without telling anyone. If a sorceress attacked, Opal would be defenseless. She tried to project confidence in her voice, shouting, "Who are you? Show yourself."

The trees rustled again, and a woman's voice, fine as silk, said, "You're pointing your bow in the wrong direction. If you'd like me to show myself, put all of your weapons down."

Opal narrowed her eyes and adjusted the bow, pointing it in the direction of the voice. "How do I know you won't attack me once I'm disarmed?"

The woman laughed and metal clinked just before a large black belt flew out of the trees and thudded to the dirt. From the pockets of the fallen belt, the light-gray metal of knives, a sword, and the tip of a spear glinted in the moonlight. "There. Now it's your turn."

Opal knew it would be foolish to try to hit something she couldn't see, so she complied. She placed her bow and quiver on the forest floor. "I've put them down, but I'm keeping them within reach—so don't try anything funny."

The voice went silent for a moment. Then, she clicked her tongue in disapproval. "I said *all* of your weapons. That means the sword and knife, as well." The feminine voice sounded familiar, but Opal couldn't place it.

She put down her sword, which growled in protest. "There. Now, mind telling me who you are and why you're here?"

"Gladly," the woman's voice trilled. Then there was a ripple of magic from within the treetops. In one lithe movement, a young woman leapt to the ground. It looked like she'd appeared from thin air. Cloaking magic was difficult for a sorceress. *Who was she?*

The woman was clad in black leather hunting clothes. Her hair was like midnight with a halo of curls surrounding her face. Her stormy, sapphire eyes and warm umber skin glowed in the moonlight.

Recognition flashed across Opal's face. She couldn't recall the woman's name, but Opal would recognize that face anywhere. The woman was the leader of the Sorceress Clan.

Opal's hands itched to reach for the bow, but curiosity stopped her. *If she means me or my clan harm, why would she come alone?* Instinct made her recoil as the woman assessed Opal, scanning her up and down.

When the woman noticed, she laughed and said, "Why are you the one that looks scared? I'm the one that snuck into enemy territory with no backup."

Opal started. She hadn't expected the sorceress to be so forthright. Still, Opal couldn't trust the sorceress. Everyone knew they lied. "Why are you here?"

The woman smiled at that. "Not even going to ask my name, huh? Just straight to the point. Well, my name is Joan. I was the leader of the Sorceress Clan, but the Council overthrew me. I'm here to keep them from stealing the sword in the stone." Joan's lip quirked in an awkward half-smile.

Opal gasped. The enchantresses and the sorceresses had been fighting over that sword for years, but Opal never thought they would go so far as to try to steal it.

The last war waged over Excalibur reduced both clans' lands to rubble. The remaining elemental mages fled to the human world. The air in the ruined villages was tainted with dark magic that choked the life out of all who entered them. Opal's heart dropped into her stomach. That couldn't happen to her clan.

"Why did you come here?"

"To warn you. My people have crossed a line, and I refuse to support them. I can help stop them."

Opal shifted uncomfortably. She had a feeling her people

would be more likely to shoot first and ask questions later if Joan was spotted on their land.

Joan moved closer and extended her hand. "Allies?"

Opal didn't take Joan's hand. Touching Joan's palms, her conduit of magic, could be fatal—especially as a sorceress powerful enough to lead a clan. Sorceress magic was deadly on the skin, but Opal's magic, enchantress magic, would only affect gems, not people. She was at a disadvantage if they touched. Opal eyed Joan skeptically, and Joan's smile fell. She dropped her outstretched hand.

Opal gave a sheepish grin. "Nothing personal. I'm just being cautious." Opal scooped up her weapons and strapped them back on without taking her eyes off of Joan. "But I'll help you." Opal tossed her cloak at Joan. "If you want to help my clan, take this. We can't have them learning your identity unless you want to become a sorceress-kebab." Opal gave Joan a shrewd look. "Keep the hood on and your head down."

Opal and Joan snuck through the village. Most people's lights were off, but those that were still awake spotted Opal and gave her a look of disgust before drawing their curtains.

Joan threw a questioning glance at Opal. "Why are they so wary of our presence? Do they recognize me?" Joan bit down on a fingernail.

Opal gave Joan a sheepish look. "It's not you they're wary of."

Joan opened her mouth in an *O* but didn't question Opal further. Joan reached out and gave Opal's shoulder a light squeeze. "I'm sorry to hear that."

Opal flinched at Joan's touch but relaxed when she didn't feel a spark of pain. Her gaze kept darting to the former enemy at her side as they took the route to the only person that might help them. Coral took joy in defying the social norms everyone else clung to. She might take Opal's side just to spite the rest of the town.

Opal had heard rumors about Coral's feud with her parents.

Some said it was about her mother's spell work, and others thought her mother had betrayed the clan in the past. Opal wasn't sure what to believe.

Her parents' rejection at her Choosing still stung. She'd gone through the trouble of finding a strong gem only to be denied the things she wanted: respect and acceptance.

Siding with Coral would upset Opal's parents and help Joan. Perfect.

As Opal and Joan approached Coral's home, they found a dim lantern lighting the front porch, giving hope that the old woman was still awake. Opal rapped on the door. "Coral, are you there?"

Coral's salmon-colored hair and wrinkled face peeked out from her door. When she saw Opal, Coral smiled. "Please come in, dear, and bring your friend as well. I've been expecting you."

Opal beckoned Joan inside, but Joan's feet were rooted to the ground. Coral must have sensed Joan's apprehension because Coral said, "Don't worry. I don't bite." Joan's shoulders relaxed slightly, and she entered the tiny hut.

Once they were in Coral's home, she turned to Opal and frowned. "If *you're* coming to me, that means there must be a threat to our clan. Tell me why you've brought a sorceress to my door tonight."

Joan looked up at that. "How did you…"

Coral smiled. "I knew before you entered my home. The fact that Opal covered your face told me as much. A spell to alter your appearance would be better. Hiding your face makes it obvious that you aren't one of our kind. But before I help you, I want to know your intentions." Joan opened her mouth to speak, but Coral put a finger to Joan's lips. "Not with your mouth child, with your heart."

Coral infused some magic into a rose quartz and placed it in Joan's hand. Coral's hand shook as she handed over the stone. Quartz could be hard to master if it wasn't your affinity.

The stone glowed a rosy pink and then turned white in Joan's hands. Coral nodded, as if the gem's behavior was exactly what she expected.

"What does that mean?" Joan asked.

"It means your intentions are pure," replied Coral with a smile.

Joan dropped the stone, and it fell to the floor. "You can tell all of that just from a gem?"

Coral cracked a smile. "Why, of course. I am an elder after all." Coral took out a small piece of unpolished alexandrite and muttered a few words as she passed her hand over the stone. She began wrapping it in silver wire.

Opal watched Coral as she worked. "Remind me again why you don't like my mother? Not that I'm against your help, but I've heard so many rumors. What's the real reason?"

Coral scratched her head. "Well, I used to be the clan leader until she challenged me. Also, the damn woman mumbles her spells. I hate that. Learn to enunciate."

Opal held up her hand. "Wait, wait, wait. Did you just say you used to be the leader?"

Coral nodded. "Yes, I did. That is, until your snake of a mother took that title from under my nose. Now, I just annoy her in any way possible to get under her skin as payback. I guess you can say I'm a sore loser."

Opal shook her head. *No wonder she wants to piss off my parents.*

Coral looped a silver chain through the wire cage and turned the alexandrite necklace over in her fingers as she spoke. "Wear this around your neck. Just like the gem itself, the spell allows your eyes to change color when exposed to light. In the light, your eyes will be purple, a common color for enchantresses. That should help keep you hidden. Just don't lose it."

Coral handed the necklace to Joan. Joan tried to put on the gem herself, but she kept fumbling with the clasp.

Opal held out her hand to help. Joan blushed, and deposited the necklace into Opal's hand. Opal sat behind Joan. Opal's fingers brushed Joan's neck as she swept Joan's hair aside. When the clasp finally hooked, Opal gasped at the sudden change.

"Can I see?" Joan asked, and the old woman handed Joan a mirror.

Opal marveled at how different Joan looked with purple eyes. Her cheekbones stood out more, and her skin matched well with violet eyes. She'd fit right in. It was unsettling how powerful the enchantment was. She looked like a different person.

Opal turned to Coral and said, "Thank you for the help. Any chance you could convince the clan to listen to us?"

Coral shook her head. "I'm afraid I can't. If we tell them Joan is here, they'll try to kill her. If one of you is chosen by the sword in the stone, then maybe they'll listen. They'll worship anyone that it chooses, but I'm afraid it hasn't chosen someone in hundreds of years."

Joan's grip on the pendant tightened, and she turned to Coral. "Tell us where the sword is. If they can't accept our word, I'll retrieve Excalibur myself." Opal and Coral turned to Joan with a puzzled look. Joan gave a sour smile. "I'm the reason they want to invade. Our elder foretold that I would be the one to pull the sword from the stone. The Council wants the power of the sword. They think if they control Excalibur, they can return to the old ways. They want to be the most powerful sect of magicians again."

They both stared at her, mouths agape. If Joan's elder was right, she would be the first sorceress to ever pull the sword from the stone. A flare of jealousy settled in Opal's stomach. She was a pariah, rejected by her own clan. That would explain why the Fire Opal was so willing to bind with her, though. *How much of it was her desire versus her fate?*

Opal grabbed Joan's hand. "Let's go."

Coral followed close behind as they crept through the town.

It was late enough that most people's lights were off. The alexandrite pendant glowed softly in the darkness. After passing several mismatched buildings with walls made of stone, brick, and concrete, they finally passed by Opal's own home.

Attached to her family's personal armory was a giant safe. Excalibur would be waiting for them at its center, but first they had to slip in unnoticed.

They peered through the windows near the entrance gate. The weapons glittered in the moonlight, tempting her from their displays. Strong protection magic pressed down on her.

She worried two people couldn't be powerful enough to disarm the enchantments. Joan certainly wouldn't be able to disarm them. Three of the most powerful gems of their clan were embedded in the gate. Each gemstone provided a unique layer of protection: a ruby which would set any unwanted intruders aflame; malachite enchanted by the famous Merlin, which would crack and curse those who entered forcibly; even a few lapis lazuli. Those enchantments were vicious and could render someone a mindless shell. These were stones appointed to the most powerful leaders their clan had seen. Some of the enchantments were over a hundred years old.

Getting in would be harder than they thought. She didn't know if her new and untrained opal magic would be enough to break these enchantments, even with the power of the familiar.

However, Coral was already working on taking out the enchantments. Her forehead beaded with sweat, plastering her orange-and-pink hair to her wrinkled skin. The malachite glowed and hissed as she worked.

If Coral was unperturbed by the sheer volume and vicious-ness of the curses on the gems before them, Opal figured she shouldn't hesitate either. While the elder muttered under her breath, Opal joined in to help with the malachite.

She didn't know any of the verbal spells, but she felt her

magic pulsing underneath her skin, waiting for her command. Her magic prodded the facets of the gem for the push of an enchantment. This one had a strange locking mechanism to it, like a puzzle box.

Several people had channeled their magic into this gem. The different shades of blue from turquoise to midnight shone like spiderwebs as she prodded the spell. She focused on disarming the enchantment one step at a time so as not to accidentally set off the gem's defenses.

Warmth spread through her hand, and her palm glowed the same silver white as her hair. She could feel each piece of the enchantment fall away, like a weight being lifted from her hands. She sighed in relief when the malachite's surface grew dull. The enchantment dissipated, but Coral and Opal both panted heavily from the exertion.

Only two more to go. She didn't know many spells, but she knew how to disarm the enchantment familiar to her, so she focused on the lapis lazuli next.

Every future clan leader learned how to create and disarm enchantments. It surprised her how quickly her magic unlocked the labyrinth-like magic of the ruby and lapis enchantments. Each successive enchantment became easier to tackle, and a contented roar from her dragon familiar vibrated through her mind. Her silver-white magic became threaded through with purple and red from her familiar. Maybe her magic was stronger than she'd thought.

After what felt like hours, drenched in sweat, they brought down the last barrier and pushed open the entrance gate. The objects locked away in this room were so powerful that they had minds of their own. The weapons chose their owners, and they were volatile and picky.

The magical objects here had a bad habit of killing enchantresses that were insolent enough to attempt to wield them. One item that caught her eye was a book the color of the night sky that radiated forbidden magic.

Take it. It belongs to you, the dragon whispered.

She shook her head. The magic in that book could corrupt and destroy even the most powerful mage, and she'd already lost enough from dabbling with dangerous magic.

She ignored the book, and they continued down the marble corridor until they spotted the sword in the stone. The Tiger's Eye in the sword's hilt shone even in the room's dim light, its glow illuminating the corridor. The sword was embedded in a large chunk of granite. Its sheath, embedded with malachite, lay next to the granite slab.

Tiger's Eye was the most powerful protection stone, and it could conjure great strength for a warrior. Excalibur's familiar was an overly aggressive tiger with a temper that could match Opal's own, and the malachite embedded in its hilt guarded it from fusing with its darker twin, Clarent.

Opal gripped her sword so hard that her fingers were turning white as Joan approached Excalibur. *Would it really choose her?* It hadn't chosen anyone in centuries, but if the sorceress's village elder predicted it, then it was probably true.

Joan crept over to the sword as if approaching a wild animal, and in a sense she was. It was a dangerous weapon that had been known to kill anyone it deemed unworthy. Joan closed her eyes as she gripped the sword.

Opal watched in awe as it slid out like someone had greased it just for this occasion.

It glowed in Joan's hands, and her jaw dropped. She suddenly flung the sword away, and it clanged to the tile floor. She exclaimed, "Am I going crazy, or did it just talk?"

Opal and Coral burst out laughing.

"What's so funny?" Joan asked, crossing her arms over her chest.

"You practice magic, but you're surprised that weapons can talk?" Opal snorted.

Joan leveled a glare at Opal. "Well, no weapon has ever spoken to *me* before. Maybe that's normal for you, but for *me* it's rather strange." Joan picked the sword back up with some hesitation and cringed before mumbling, "Sorry. I didn't know."

She grabbed the nearby sheath with a small, rounded malachite at its center and fastened both to her belt. "Now what?" she asked, her head cocked to one side in question.

"Now, we hope my parents and the rest of the clan will listen to reason. I'll take you to them in the morning."

CHAPTER THREE

Coral helped gather the clan the next morning by claiming she'd seen their clan's future. When they gathered around, she said, "Enchantress Clan! I had a vision that a sorceress would seek our help, and last night she arrived." Murmurs could be heard pulsing through the crowd.

Opal stifled a laugh when a grumpy male enchanter yelled, "Why would one of *them* need our help? I thought we were inferior magicians."

Coral glared at him. "She seeks our help in stopping the Sorceress Clan from invading our land, as we've feared." Several people gasped, and the murmuring got louder.

Joan emerged from Coral's hut to address the crowd. "That's why I want to help you stop them!" she said, brandishing her sword for the whole clan to see.

A twinge of respect and jealousy warred within Opal as the clan bent to Joan's will. Seeing Excalibur and its shining Tiger's Eye was enough to make them listen. Opal wished she had that kind of power at her fingertips.

The clan she was meant to rule had rejected her so easily, but they'd accepted one of their enemies to lead them because she had Excalibur. Opal was getting sick of her clan's blind reliance on prophecies and visions to make decisions. After this battle, she would abolish such nonsense and chastise the people who relied on omens so heavily as treasonous simpletons.

Once Joan had hyped the clan up for the coming battle, Opal tuned back in. "We will face the sorceresses in a week's time. We will tell them that we will not take their treason lying down. They'll have two choices: join us or perish at the hands of our swords and bows."

A cheer erupted from the crowd. Some of the children, with tears in their eyes, gripped their toy swords tighter in their hands. Even Opal felt a tear form in her eye, but she brushed it aside.

It was a good time for her to take the stage as the clan leader.

"They planned to steal our most prized weapon from us, and for what? Greed and pride? They think they can take what they want, but we will show them the price of such selfish thinking. Let's ready our weaponry and mobilize our horses for the coming fight. Children, and men without familiars, will be left behind. Men with familiars will join the battle or stay back as support. Women, we will ride into battle together."

The clan hesitated to react to her words until Joan grabbed Opal's hand and said, "We'll beat them together."

One of the younger enchantresses, a girl with short blond hair and her hands on her hips, chimed in with, "We don't want to hear from you. You're not a leader. A leader wouldn't abandon their Choosing because of a bad prophecy. They would face it head on." Whispers spread through the crowd like a wildfire. Opal opened her mouth to give a retort, but she didn't have to.

Joan's face darkened, and she sauntered over to the girl and gripped her arm in a vice. "That sounds an awful lot like treason, girl. Do you know what happens to people who commit treason where I'm from?" The girl blinked her wide eyes and shook her head. Joan flashed a sardonic grin. "They get jailed… or executed. Is that what you want?"

The girl's face went white, and she said weakly, "No."

Joan's tone went flat. "Then show your leader respect." Joan turned her gaze to the crowd.

After a moment of pause, the clan gave a lackluster cheer before rushing off to prepare.

Opal was glad to have Joan's support, even if it made Opal a little jealous. She clenched and unclenched her hand, breathing a deep sigh. Joan leaned in close to Opal's ear. "It takes a lot of courage to fight for your beliefs when your clan has lost faith in you. When the Council defied me, I ran instead of fighting."

Opal's mouth opened in shock, but the validation made her stand taller. Joan was the type of leader Opal had always wanted to be. She hoped she could command her troops when the time came.

She would just have to earn her clan's respect on the battle-field. That was one place where she knew she'd feel at home.

Coral turned back to Opal and Joan. "We've managed to mobilize the clan. Now, we need to figure out what we're going to do when the sorceresses arrive. They outnumber us five to one. If they come in full force, there's a good chance they'll wipe us out."

Opal grinned. With what Joan had said last night, talking into the early morning hours, Opal knew just what to do. "Get me the enchantresses most skilled at barrier magic. Amethysts and other quartz affinities would be best. I'll explain once they join us."

After a few hours, Coral returned with a group of enchantresses.

Two of the recruits stood out from the group.

One was a girl with golden eyes and short, cropped black hair. She stood several feet closer to Opal and watched every-one's lips intently. The girl's baggy clothing hid her silhouette, and she wore two sports bras to flatten her chest. She wore no jewelry and no makeup. Strange. Her golden eyes watched Opal's lips intently. The girl gripped a brown stone with a swirling yellow pattern, a calligraphy script stone. She was almost a head shorter than Opal.

A short young girl with violet hair radiated powerful magic that sparked around her like electricity. The girl's chin tilted up in defiance, and an amethyst bracelet on her wrist glowed with the light of a familiar. A Choosing didn't happen until age eighteen, but the girl's short stature and the sparkly purple scrunchy on her wrist suggested she was twelve at the oldest. *She couldn't be that girl, could she?*

Opal leaned closer to Coral and nodded to the purple-haired girl. "Is she who I think she is?"

Coral's eyes widened in understanding. "Yes, that's Amy. The one that made local news. She completed her Choosing ceremony at ten. She's apt in both barrier and cloaking magic. However, she still struggles to control her magic."

Opal pursed her lips. "Interesting. We'll train her to cloak our forces as well then. She could be useful." Opal clapped Coral on the shoulder and then approached the girl. "Amethyst, you're going to have an important job in this battle, so I need you to behave, okay?"

The girl glared at Opal. "That's not my name. I'm Amy." The girl huffed and put her hands on her hips.

Opal prickled at the girl's disrespect, but Opal did her best to hide her annoyance with a tight-lipped smile. "Sorry… Amy. I'm going to train you, okay?" Amy smiled at the use of her name, revealing a missing baby tooth.

Seeing how young she was up close made Opal uneasy. Hopefully, they could stop the sorceresses' army before the girls got into real danger. Opal stepped away from Amy and strode back to stand by Joan.

Now, the debriefing would begin.

Opal took a few deep breaths to steady herself before turning to speak to the group. She needed to sound confident or they wouldn't follow her. They were already distrustful of her as it was. Opal straightened her back and lifted her chin, channeling the booming voice her father used to command their army.

"Listen up. We need to keep this battle from turning into a war. Joan and I will try to negotiate with the sorceresses, but to do that we'll need your help. You're going to create a barrier to protect us, so they have a chance to hear us out. Any questions?"

Opal wondered if maybe the amber-eyed girl was deaf from the way she'd been watching Opal's lips. She signed, "Questions?" and the girl's eyes lit up.

Joan leaned over and touched a hand to Opal's shoulder. "Learning another language for your people. Color me impressed."

Opal blushed. "Well, ten percent of our population uses sign language." She was glad she'd studied it in school. Her skills were finally of use to her clan.

Joan's response was pained. "If only my clan thought like that." She moved back to her spot behind Opal.

The girl with violet hair raised her hand. "Who will be leading the charge into battle? You or the sorceress?" Her hands rested on her hips and her foot tapped impatiently. Opal felt a pinch of jealousy and wondered if Coral had lured them here with the promise of being led by Joan, the one chosen by the sword.

Opal sighed mentally before responding, "We will be leading the charge together. Any other questions?" They were silent, and Opal looked over her shoulder to see Joan approach. They stared at her, eyes wide with admiration, and Opal's jealousy pricked at her once again.

When Joan passed by and saw Opal's expression, Joan gave

Opal's shoulder a light squeeze of encouragement. Opal sneered when Joan shot the purple-haired girl an icy glare.

The recruits crowded closer. Questions started bubbling to the surface, tumbling over each other and drowning one another out.

"What's it like being chosen by the sword?"

"Do you feel more powerful now that you have it?"

"What's our plan for this battle?"

Opal couldn't tell who was speaking and kept swiveling her head, trying to keep up with the conversation until Joan cut them off with a smile. "Everyone! Before we get into questions, why don't you start by telling me your names?"

The first one to speak was the violet-haired girl from before. "I'm Amy. My affinity is amethyst." Her silver-and-amethyst bracelet glowed brighter when she spoke.

Next, a waif of a girl with an intense gaze and slate-gray eyes said, "My name is Crystal, and my affinity is for crystal quartz."

A pink-haired girl next to Crystal flashed a cocky grin. "My name is Pink, but you can call me Rosie. My affinity is rose quartz."

The recruit Opal had signed to before cleared her throat. Her voice was loud and a bit rough when she spoke. "I'm Cat. I have a cat's eye affinity." Cat gripped a calligraphy stone, a communication gem, tighter and let her short, cropped black bangs fall over her eyes.

Cat's gemstone was embedded in a pocket watch that hung from the waistband of her baggy black pants. After speaking, she shoved her hands in her pockets.

A cat's eye affinity. That meant she'd be good at protection spells, especially against unknown dangers, and her gem would be great with light and bending light for illusions. She'd also be better at spotting the enemy from afar and building a sound barrier. Opal signed, "Thank you" and smiled. Cat blushed and turned away, embarrassed.

Opal had a fascination with linguistics and was glad her language-learning skills were finally coming in handy.

Opal addressed the group, signing as she spoke aloud. "Today, we are going to test the limits of your magic. Our goal is to see what your strengths are and how long you can hold a shield. Understand?"

All of them nodded, except for Cat, who raised her hand. "What happens if we can't convince them?"

Opal's smile dropped. Her gaze was solemn. "If we can't convince them, you will retreat. We will have to face them in battle, and I don't want such young lives snuffed out."

As Opal relayed this information, Pink slumped her shoulders, Crystal bit her lip, and Amy sniffled as her eyes teared up. Cat just absorbed the information without flinching or looking away. She stared at Opal and nodded in understanding.

"Cat and Amy. You're with Joan and me. Pink and Crystal. I want you to take turns making shields with Coral. Attack each other's shields to test their strength. Use all your force, and don't worry about hurting each other. Coral is an excellent healer, and so am I." Pink and Crystal nodded and moved off to the side.

Opal signed, "T-r-a-i-n-i-n-g."

Cat signed back, "With you?"

Opal nodded and then signed the words *practice*, *looking*, and *threats*. Then she moved close, making sure her lips were visible to Cat. "When you can see me, use this." Opal grabbed a celestine, a flare gem, from her pocket and channeled her magic into it. She threw the gem up as high as she could, and when it sailed over the treetops, it sparked into a large red flame.

Opal handed Cat a few more celestines for that day's practice. Then without another word, Opal ran into the forest and hid.

She started as far into the forest as she could go without crossing over into sorceress territory. Opal hid behind trees and in bushes as she went. It was important to be as stealthy as possible so Cat would be prepared when the real fight took place.

After getting about halfway to camp, she saw Cat's flare go up. The red flame was tinged with a green color. *Good, but not good enough.* Opal retreated and tried again. Each time, Cat got a little faster at finding Opal. After a few tries, Cat hadn't quite reached Opal's goal of four hundred feet, but Cat had expanded her range an extra twenty feet. That would have to do.

Opal rushed back to the training grounds. She needed to check in on Crystal and Pink's training, so Opal instructed Cat to practice making a barrier in the meantime. Cat's forehead beaded with sweat. *I hope I'm not pushing them too hard,* Opal thought but brushed the thought aside. She had a task before her and needed to focus.

"Watch her while I'm gone," Opal called out to Joan. Joan gave a quick thumbs up before she walked away.

When Opal got to the other side of the clearing, Pink was striking Crystal's barrier with a rose quartz knife. Coral saw Opal approach and grabbed Pink's shoulder to stop her next attack. Crystal breathed a sigh of relief and slumped to the floor.

"Crystal. Pink. I'm going to teach you some tricks for making your barrier stronger. Then I'm going to attack you at full force to see how long your barrier holds. Any questions?"

Pink blurted out, "Are you trying to kill us?" Her arms were crossed over her chest, and she lowered a glare at Opal that would've made any first-year magic student cower in fear. Of course, Pink put on a brave face the second Joan was out of earshot.

Opal glowered at Pink in return. "First of all, that's a disrespectful way to speak to your leader. Second of all, we're doing this so you won't die in battle." Opal raised an eyebrow at the two of them. "Understand?"

Crystal nodded, but Pink said, "I wouldn't exactly call you my leader. I'd say that title belongs to Joan. You ran away from your own ceremony because of some bad prophecy." Pink smirked, as if she knew she'd hit home with that last comment. The comment stung, and Opal had to bite her lip to keep from saying something she'd regret.

It was like Pink had never grown out of her mean-girl phase even though she was nineteen years old. It was shameful, and arguing with her would be a waste of time.

Opal took a deep breath before she spoke again. "Yes, I made a mistake, but I'm here making up for it by trying to protect our clan here and now. So, let's work together because that's the only way to prepare for what's coming."

Pink nodded in acceptance and unfolded her arms.

"Now, imagine the strongest material you can, like bricks or diamonds. You're going to stack that material into a wall around you. Make that wall as strong as possible. Imagine that anyone trying to get through the wall is pushed away."

Crystal closed her eyes and started to create her wall. Opal could see the force field getting thicker as the girl clutched her small crystal quartz staff.

Opal smiled and nodded at her work, but Pink was struggling. Her shield was still the same, and her eyes were open. "Does what you're saying really work? Or are you making this up as a joke or something?"

Opal smiled. A demonstration was in order. "Crystal. Brace yourself. I'm about to attack." Opal grabbed her Fire Opal sword and slashed at Crystal's shield. The barrier spit and crackled from the impact.

The clear magic barrier knocked Opal back several feet. Just before she hit the ground, she twisted and broke the fall with her free hand.

Pink rubbed her eyes in disbelief. Crystal's mouth hung open. They were both stunned at the force of Crystal's shield.

Before Opal could give further instructions, a pillar of purple magic streamed into the sky from the other side of the clearing. A shrill scream pierced the air. It sounded like Joan.

"Wait here," Opal commanded, and she ran to the source of the purple magic. She hoped Joan and Amy were okay.

When Opal got there, Amy's eyes were wide, and her hair was mussed. She looked like a cornered animal being hunted. "I don't know what happened. She attacked my shield, and I panicked. I think it threw her back really hard. I didn't mean to hurt her." Tears fell down Amy's face.

Joan's sword had been thrown halfway across the clearing, and she was flat on her back ten feet from Amy's shield. Opal couldn't see the rise and fall of Joan's chest from this distance, and blood flowed from Joan's palms, staining the ground.

Opal tried to project a soothing voice despite her frazzled nerves. "It's alright. I'm just going to check to make sure she's okay. Sometimes this happens with training." She tried to sound reassuring, but panic twisted in her stomach.

She rushed to Joan's side and took a leaf from the ground to place it just above her mouth. The leaf moved slightly. When Opal looked closer, Joan's chest rose and fell. She was alive, but weak. Maybe Amy was too young for training after all. With wild magic like hers, she could put everyone in danger.

"Is she okay?" Amy whispered. Her voice was timid and unsure.

Irritation and anger spiked Opal's tone. "She'll live, no thanks to you. Give me some space so I can heal her." She regretted the words the moment they'd left her mouth. Amy's face fell, and she went pale and silent. Her wide eyes searched the surrounding area, looking for anything to absolve herself of blame.

Guilt pinched Opal, but what she'd said hadn't been wrong, and if the girl was going to war with them, she'd have to learn to deal with the guilt that came with hurting and possibly even killing someone. Opal told herself this was just part of learning to deal with the reality of battle. But her conscience whispered, *They wouldn't have to go into battle if you were a better leader.*

Opal brushed the thought off. She was good at healing magic, but she needed to focus. Grabbing an emerald from her pouch, she gripped it over Joan's chest.

Opal's hands grew warm as her magic flowed through the stone, and she placed the enchanted gem on Joan's chest. The magic sank into Joan, and a few painfully slow moments later, her eyes popped open, and her breaths came in heaving gasps.

"Are you okay?" Opal asked.

Joan nodded and gave a weak smile. Opal helped pull Joan to her feet, but she had to lean on Opal's shoulder to remain standing. Joan looked between Amy and Opal in turn. "I'm okay, but Amy shouldn't go into battle. She still hasn't fully mastered control over her magic."

Amy gripped the purple stone in her hand. "But I want to help. Don't I get a say in this?"

Opal's gaze softened. "Of course you do, but we want to make sure we're doing what's best for the whole clan. If you can't control your magic, someone could get seriously hurt."

Amy thought about this for a moment, her forehead creasing in thought. Then she said, "Maybe I can be there as backup, in case things go sour when we talk to the sorceresses."

Opal considered this. "Okay. For the rest of the day, we'll switch places. I will train you to your limits. You need to know how to control your magic. If anything happens, I'll make sure you regret it." Joan nodded, and Cat came to help Joan walk over to Coral. As they walked away, Opal dug her nails into her palm. *Amy almost killed Joan and still wanted to go into battle. I'll make her regret that decision.*

"After today, you're going to wish you'd backed out of this battle." She gripped her Fire Opal sword in her hand and channeled as much energy as possible. "I'm going to train you until you want to collapse, and then we'll continue until you actually collapse. You'd better not harm a hair on anyone's head on the day of the battle. Otherwise, I will personally throw you into the dungeon. Understand?"

Amy nodded and assumed a defensive stance. Opal gave Amy no time to think before charging at her shield, bracing herself for the recoil of hitting Amy's magic.

But Opal's weapon crackled as it grew closer to the shield, and the shield dissipated with a pop before her. Opal's mouth dropped open in shock. *Maybe her own power was what they needed to worry about.* She had to stop herself so she wouldn't run right into Amy.

Tossing her thoughts aside, Opal said, "Again," and tried once more. The shield held up a little better, but like before, the magic of her sword broke through.

Amy grew weaker each time, but Opal was determined to test her strength against this girl. She wanted—no, needed—to keep fighting. Her vision was edged in red that grew brighter the longer she fought. It wasn't until Joan came over and grabbed Opal's arm that she noticed the damage she'd done.

Amy was curled up in a ball on the forest floor. Her skin was dotted with blue and purple. One of her eyes was swollen shut. Amy's head tilted down as though she couldn't bear to look at Opal. *Did I do this?* Opal had gone far beyond just training. She'd been known to get lost in the heat of battle, but this had been all-out brutality. Something in her mind purred. *Battle, fight, kill. This is your purpose. Keep going.*

Opal shivered. *Is this why the townspeople fear me? Is this the darkness of my weapon, or is it my own darkness?* Either way, she needed to know more about her weapon before she used it again.

CHAPTER FOUR

When Opal got home, she headed straight for the library. After sifting through the shelves on opal magic, she still hadn't found one that matched the description for her familiar. None spoke of a Fire Opal, aside from the book with the missing pages. She couldn't find a single book on dragon familiars, and there was nothing that talked about a Fire Opal sword. The longer she kept at it, the more the cordoned-off section of the library called out to her.

The gems set in the gate, blocking the forbidden books of the library, were all quartz magic. She would just add this broken rule to her list of transgressions. The rest of the library hadn't turned up anything useful about her familiar. The restricted section was her next best bet.

Opal focused her magic on the gems, hovering her hand over one at a time. Her silver-and-red magic washed over the amethyst first and then the crystal quartz, destroying the spells that kept intruders out one by one.

After making swift work of the wards, she clicked open the gate. Her parents used this section to house dangerous and ancient magic that they couldn't control or understand.

She scoured the shelves, looking for anything about a Fire Opal, but found nothing. But a small statue of a dragon caught her attention. She spotted a small seam, revealing a secret compartment underneath its head.

A slim book was inside. The book's edges were frayed, and the cover had some scuff marks. It even looked like there were faint burns marks on its cover. The title read, *The Legend of Clarent, the Silver Sword*. Opal looked down at her own sword. It glowed. *My sword can't be Clarent, can it?* She took the glowing as a sign and grabbed the book.

She replaced the dragon's head and looked around before tucking the book into her cloak. After checking to make sure she wasn't being watched, she snuck out of the ancient magic section. Opal took care to make sure the gate didn't creak as she shut the door behind her and painstakingly stretched up to touch the gems on the gate. She channeled energy into them, trying to replicate the same twists and turns in the puzzle-like magic that the gems had held before she'd disarmed them.

Her vision blurred, and when she was done, she swayed on her feet. Her breath came in heaving gasps. Once she was confident with her handiwork, she crept over to a part of the house that only she used, her study. Every inch of wall space was covered in books, and there was a lone, suede-covered, cobalt-blue lounge chair.

She sank into the comfortable chair, but when she opened the book, a spark of magic shocked her. Opal dropped it in surprise. With some hesitation, she picked it up and opened it again. She felt a tingle of magic at her fingertips, but no shock.

Within the book's pages, she read, *Those chosen by the Silver Sword are doomed to ruin and exile. The dragon that sleeps within it has a rage that knows no bounds. Everything that person holds dear is likely to be burnt up in its wake.*

Her hands shook as she pored over the words. This had

never been covered in magic history class. The last line echoed what Coral had said on Opal's Choosing day.

An illustration in the book stopped her cold. A woman with gray hair, gray eyes, and a villainous smile stroked the scales of a dragon. *Her dragon.* The figure stood over a dead woman with dark curly hair and eyes like a stormy sea. She looked just like Joan. It was so realistic that Opal felt the dragon would jump off the page and burn her skin. She slammed the book shut, her breaths coming fast.

She couldn't allow herself to become like that, no matter what. She had to keep this dragon's rage caged. It couldn't be allowed to control her. Opal felt around for the loose floorboard underneath her chair. Pushing the floorboard up, she hid the book. She didn't want anyone else to see this, not when tensions were already high. She was too afraid to continue reading the book and learn what else its pages held.

She took a deep breath and went to her room. She fell to the mattress in her training clothes despite being covered in sweat. The book could wait until the morning.

She'd just fallen into a dreamless sleep when alarm bells woke her. It was still dark outside, but when she looked out her window, the army was already marching into the forest. In the distance, she could see the sparks of magic exploding as they collided.

Her eyes were wide with panic as realization hit her. The sorceresses had attacked early. Her clan, the children, and Joan were in danger. Opal needed to hurry.

Opal stepped out of her training gear and grabbed the enchanted leather armor from her closet. She got dressed as fast as possible, strapped her weapons on, and rushed off. She was gasping for air by the time she made it outside and saw her forest on fire. Red pushed at the edges of her vision, but she shoved it down. She wouldn't let the anger control her. She needed a level head if they were going to escape this without massive bloodshed. But first she had to find Joan and the others.

Opal ran toward the training area, searching for them, and found them halfway there.

The recruits trailed behind Joan who still had a bad case of bedhead. Amy's bruises had turned from purple to a faded yellow. That must've been Coral's handiwork.

Cat carried a moonstone emanating a bright silver glow against the surrounding darkness.

Joan rushed up to Opal and gathered her in a hug. "We're glad you're okay. We were all worried when you rushed off last night."

Cat tugged on Opal's sleeve. "I'm happy you're okay," she signed.

Joan said, "Cat couldn't sleep and saw the army approaching. She alerted Tiger and Iolite standing guard. If it weren't for her, we wouldn't have known until it was too late."

Cat slouched, shrinking down at Joan's words. Cat looked upset, but maybe Opal imagined it.

"Good job, Cat," Opal signed. Cat smiled back at Opal in return.

Joan moved closer to Opal's ear, so close that Opal blushed, her cheek warming from Joan's breath. Joan whispered, "You might not think it, but they care about you. They were worried when you left training earlier." She hesitated. "I was worried about you too." The admission was so soft, Opal almost couldn't catch it.

Joan gave Opal's arm a light squeeze. Opal was glad they'd joined forces. She only hoped they could make it out of this. She didn't want them to come to any harm, but that might not be possible at this point. If they were changing their plan of attack, the sorceresses' army might be too desperate and angry to listen.

Opal turned to Crystal. "Have you seen Topaz and Tanzanite?"

Crystal raised an eyebrow and looked over at Pink. Pink placed a hand on her hips. "Not that I'm your parents' keeper or anything, but last I saw them, they were getting the troops ready for battle."

Opal sighed in relief. "Thank you." They needed to move, and fast. Opal straightened her back. "Crystal, Pink, Amy, go over to the armory and get armored up. Pink, make sure to change out of your pajamas." Pink gave Opal a mock salute. Opal rolled her eyes and continued. "When you're finished, meet me back here, but be quick. We need to head straight for the front lines."

Some of their faces paled, but they nodded in agreement and shuffled off, except for Cat, who was already dressed in black leather armor and held a tiny crossbow. The bolts were tipped in cat's eye gems. *Interesting—a long-range weapons user, like me.* Opal signed, "Wait here," and Cat nodded.

A few minutes later, the recruits rushed back. Some were in leather armor studded with gems. Pink had opted for steel armor studded with selenite, an interesting choice. Opal hadn't pictured Pink as a stealthy fighter, considering her loud personality, but first impressions could be deceiving. Selenite was a good camouflaging gem.

"Alright. Let's move out!" Opal said once they were all together, and they headed toward the battlefield.

They fell into step behind Joan. Opal heard loud crunching behind her. She whirled around and found Cat, oblivious to the amount of noise she made. Opal had completely forgotten Cat. Before she could get too far, Opal signed, "Whiskers. S-p-e-l-l."

Cat nodded in recognition and grabbed the pocket watch hanging from her jeans. The cat's eye gem glowed a bright green, and Opal could feel magic fanning out around them. Cat removed her shoes so her feet could touch the ground and put her shoes into a pack.

After that, Cat made less noise. She cringed when she felt the crunching happening underneath her feet and adjusted. Opal reached back and grabbed Cat's hand to help guide her, and she took it, falling into step just behind Opal. Cat handed off her glowing moonstone to Joan to free up her hand.

Opal faced forward again. Her face scrunched up in concern until Joan whispered, "Have more confidence in yourself," and reached out to squeeze Opal's free arm. Opal straightened her back as they headed up to the front line.

The other soldiers in the village moved aside, giving them a clear path into the forest. Joan turned to face their group. "Be ready for anything and put that shield up the second we get into the forest," Joan boomed in a voice Opal hadn't thought Joan was capable of. They nodded, and as they entered the forest, Opal felt the shield go up.

Moments after the shield went up, a stray arrow hit it. Amy and Crystal recoiled in surprise at the sizzling and popping sound the shield made when the magics collided. This chat might prove even more difficult than they'd expected if shots were already being fired.

Cat's moonstone glowed dimly in Joan's hand, lighting their way. Thankfully, once Crystal put her cloaking spell up, the light wouldn't be visible. Until then, they'd have to try to stay out of sight.

Once they were in the forest, they would need to be as quiet as possible. She turned to Cat and signed, "Quiet." Cat nodded and put a finger to her mouth to make sure the others understood what Opal wanted.

As they crept forward, they kept their steps light. After the first incident with the arrow, Cat pointed out enemies that were getting too close, and they moved to avoid the sorceress clan's soldier, weaving through the forest underbrush.

Opal's group passed some enchantresses that had fallen in the battle already, taking arrows to the chest or a sword to the neck. Silent tears streamed down Opal's face, and some of the girls gasped in shock. They couldn't stop, but she mourned their losses as she moved on.

They pushed forward through the forest, seeing more carnage as they neared the source of the battle. The indigo-and-violet uniforms of the enchantresses' army loomed like storm clouds. From afar a sorcerer skewered an enchantress on his sword. Opal choked back a cry.

The enchantress looked about eighteen, and the sorcerer appeared even younger. Opal turned around, urging the group forward. She put a finger to her lips, reminding them to remain quiet despite the gruesome sights.

"Back. Out of sight," Opal signed to Cat, who shooed everyone backward, making sure they wouldn't be seen while Joan and Opal spoke with the sorceresses' army.

Opal signed to Cat, "Cloak." Cat grabbed her calligraphy stone from her pack. It glowed. and the words *cloaking spell* appeared in the air. Crystal nodded in understanding.

When they looked down, they could no longer see themselves. They'd have to be careful not to get hit by any stray projectiles, as that would reveal their position to the enemies.

After a few moments, the person leading the charge came into view. Red tassels dangled from his helmet, revealing his high rank. Opal shooed her troops, making sure they were hidden amongst the trees and bushes of the forest before she spoke. "We're here. Drop the cloak."

Crystal dropped the spell, and the sorceresses' army gazed at Joan in shock as they came into view.

Joan turned to the army, her gaze icy. "Stop this senseless violence, now. The sword has chosen me, and this battle is pointless. I already have what you came here for." Joan brandished the sword as proof. It glowed a bright gold in response.

For a moment, they went silent. Then some of the soldiers started arguing.

"If she's here, then why are we fighting?"

"We sacrificed our children for this?"

"Is our Council acting against our leader?"

"Enough! This girl must be an imposter. She abandoned her own people and sides with the enemy. You're going to believe her? No. She needs to be killed for her crimes and for impersonating our leader. She's not the real Joan."

A shudder went through the crowd. Some of the soldiers started to protest, but they were silenced by other people in the crowd. One soldier piped up with, "But the sword chose her. She can't be an imposter, right?"

The leader smirked. "Clearly, the sword is also a fake."

Joan whispered to the sword, "Now would be a good time to show them your true power—whatever that is." But nothing happened. Joan bit her lip. "It's true that I fled the Council and our clan. I went seeking help when I knew they planned to attack this village. But I am no traitor, and this sword is no fake."

At that moment, the sword released a large pillar of golden magic into the air and through their barrier.

The soldiers looked uncertainly between Joan and their commander, who shook his head angrily. "I'll prove she's a liar!" He raised his sword against Joan, but his sword smacked into the shield instead. Amy screamed in shock when the sword hit. Opal froze. *Please don't let her lose control again.*

The shield sparked, and the man shook like he'd been struck by lightning. He flew back with such force that his body slammed against a tree. The sound echoed all around. He fell to the forest floor, dead.

Amy rushed out from her hiding spot. "I'm so sorry." Tears ran down her face. The other soldiers looked down in horror at what happened.

"Our leader wouldn't put children in danger."

"She wouldn't kill her own people," the crowd murmured.

One soldier from the pack came forward. "Are we going to trust the people that just killed our leader and endangered children, or are we going to fight?"

A chorus came from the crowd, "Fight!"

Opal's eyes widened in panic. She turned toward the hiding spot in the trees. "Amy, Crystal, Pink, and Cat. Keep this shield up, but only for you. Leave us behind and run back to town. You'll be safe there." Pink and Crystal opened their mouths to protest, but Opal's voice turned steely. "Now!"

They made an opening for Joan and Opal to exit the shield and ran. Cat gave one last look back, her forehead wrinkled in concern. Cat had Amy in tow, hauling her by the elbow.

"Ready?" Opal said as she turned to Joan.

"If this battle is with you, I'll gladly lay down my life," Joan said with a smile. She snapped her fingers, forming two orbs of magic so hot they were deep blue and launched them toward the soldiers' horses.

The acrid scent of char assaulted Opal's nose. The horses whinnied and bucked, trying to flee the flames. Opal brandished her sword and knife and wove through the mounted soldiers to immobilize those fighting on the ground. She tossed a snakestone that was enchanted to make rattling noises. The threat of a predator nearby made the remaining horses scatter.

As Opal pushed through the crowd, she lost sight of Joan. Panic seized Opal. An arrow flew toward her, and she didn't have enough time to block it. She braced herself for the blow, but her familiar appeared with a roar, blocking the arrow with its massive body. Fire built in its belly, and it exhaled white fire on the sorceresses' army. Several shielded themselves, but many more were barbequed by the fire.

Opal pushed forward, slowly moving too far away to help Joan. Turning her back to the enemy would surely get her killed. She kept moving, shooting arrows from the enchanted short bow that had been strapped to her back. Her opal dragon familiar hovered in front of her, mowing down threats.

When an enemy got too close, she slashed out with her obsidian knife. All she really cared about was the safety of her friends. She hoped Cat and the others had made it back to the village without any issues. Time felt like it moved too quickly, and Opal struggled to keep her focus on the battle.

That loss of focus cost her. An arrow sunk into her right eye, and she screeched in pain. Her body burned as its tip buried into her eye socket. Her first instinct was to remove the arrow, but she knew that could be a deadly mistake. The dragon roared in anger, lashing out to attack anyone nearby.

When her dragon saw the man that had pierced her eye, it tore him from the tree with its teeth, ripping into his flesh. A chill ran down Opal's spine, overwhelming the searing pain.

There was a chance Coral could heal the eye later. Trying to remove the arrow could cause more damage.

She took some deep, heaving breaths to steady herself. She sliced off the end of the arrow to make it easier to move. Her body screamed in pain from the movement as the arrow shifted in her eye socket.

She grabbed a clear quartz from her pack and focused on removing some of her pain and channeling it into this blank slate of a gem. When the pain had sufficiently dulled, she tucked the gem back into the pack.

Footsteps crushed a leaf behind her. She readied her knife and lashed out at the source of the noise but stopped herself, inches from the person's neck, when she recognized the curly dark hair and stormy blue eyes. It was Joan.

Joan fell to her knees. Panting. She had several gaping wounds and punctures in her legs. It looked like she'd been hit several times on her way here. "Are you okay? I heard you scre

—" She stopped short, eyes wide, when she saw the remaining piece of the arrow in Opal's eye.

"It's okay," Opal said. "It's my eye, not my life."

But Joan wasn't listening anymore. Rage came off her in waves, and her magic surged in deep-blue tumults. Her eyes ran through with gold, the same color as her sword's magic.

"The Magic Council and all of their supporters will pay for their actions, now." The sapphire-and-gold ball of magic grew to the size of a person in her palm. It grew larger and larger.

"Joan. What are you doing? What happened to trying to settle this with as little bloodshed as possible? Remember, these people aren't the Council. They didn't start this."

Joan tensed her shoulders and spoke through gritted teeth, "They had their chance to settle this peacefully. They've hurt and killed my comrades." She stared intently at Opal. "They don't deserve to walk away from this unscathed. If they want a fight, let's give them one."

Opal's jaw went slack. Seeing Joan like this sent a chill down Opal's spine. She moved, blocking Joan's way forward. "I won't let you do this. You'll only regret it later. Let's face the Magic Council directly. They're the ones that caused this mess. They're the ones that deserve to pay."

Joan nodded, but her gaze was still haunted. The magic in her palm shrank until it was just a candle's flame of blue fire. The gold magic was gone.

Her eyes had gone back to normal, but her expression was hollow, defeated.

Opal moved closer and grabbed onto Joan's shoulder. Joan leaned into Opal. "When I tried to stop their invasion… They sent a mercenary after me. That's why I escaped to your land. They need to pay."

Opal's shoulders tensed. They couldn't just waltz into the Council's room. It could end up being a suicide mission if they weren't careful. Opal turned to address the soldiers. "You just saw the extent of Joan's power, and I'm sure you don't want to die in a dragon's inferno either. Move and your lives will be spared—for now."

At first, the sorceresses just stared at each other, but one by one they started to move. Her dragon continued to curl around her and Joan protectively as they moved forward.

Opal found it rather strange for her familiar to transform in battle like that. Typically, they wouldn't act in battle unless given orders. This was something she would need to research later, along with the sword in the stone.

Despite having what was supposed to be the most powerful sword, Joan was covered in wounds from small magic and arrows alike. *What was the sword good for aside from swinging around?* Although, after seeing the gold threaded through her magic earlier, Opal wondered if maybe the sword enhanced Joan's magic.

Opal reached out and grabbed Joan's hand, giving it a light squeeze. Joan shook it off and gave a slight smile, but it held no warmth. She had a one-track mind, and nothing Opal did or said was going to change that. Opal couldn't say she blamed Joan after what the Council had done, but Opal wasn't fond of the idea of hurting any more people. Despite her tendency to anger quickly, she wasn't a huge fan of violence, and she'd had her fill of it that day.

As they continued through the forest, a large gray stone castle surrounded by a barrier appeared through the thicket of trees. Opal could tell from the spiral pillars, ancient stone walls, and massive stained-glass windows that the Sorceress Clan's leaders preferred the older type of architecture here. This looked like a castle from the sixteenth century, not the twenty-first.

They approached the barrier, and Joan grabbed Opal's hand. Warmth spread through her, and an unusual power filled her.

Then, they passed through the barrier without a problem. She gave Joan a questioning gaze.

"It's designed to keep out those without sorceress magic, so I transferred some magic to you to get you through the barrier." That must've been the warmth Opal had felt. She didn't know magic could be transferred like that, but she guessed it didn't last long. Unlike gems, people weren't good at holding unfamiliar magic in their bodies.

As they crept closer, Joan tensed. Opal grabbed Joan's hand and threaded their fingers together. "It'll be okay. We're in this together."

Joan turned to Opal. "I hope you're right."

As Opal followed Joan to the Council room, Opal didn't see any guards. Strange. She'd imagined that even in war someone would've been left to protect their figureheads.

An uneasy feeling settled in Opal's stomach. Maybe they were walking into a trap. She didn't have time to think about it further, though, as Joan pushed the Council room's door open. Their enemy was before them. Opal followed Joan, running through the door just a moment later.

Three men and a woman sat in gold-leafed thrones encrusted in rubies, sapphires, and emeralds. They laughed when Joan and Opal walked in.

"The mouse fell for the trap, and it brought a friend, too," a man with a forked tongue hissed.

An iron cage dropped from the ceiling, clanging over them. Opal couldn't feel the presence of her familiar any longer, and her sword reappeared at her side, but its glow was muted. Her veins felt strange, like her magic had been blocked.

"No use fighting it. This will block any of your magic," the woman with black stones for eyes said. Joan's terrified look confirmed Opal's fears. They were sitting ducks.

"Now we can kill you without any interruptionsss," the man

from before hissed. She imagined his magic being as oily as his tone of voice.

The cage was woven through with magic-dampening metals, iron and lead. One of the women closed the door and locked it with a metal key.

A tall, lean man stepped forward and said, "I'll do the honors." His eyes were a striking blue, the same color as Joan's. His nose and cheekbones had a sharpness that mirrored hers, but on him they looked cruel rather than commanding. He was too young to be her parent, but there was no question. They were related.

Joan's eyes widened in fear. Her hands gripped the cage so hard that her knuckles turned white. "Brother. You don't want to do this."

His eyes lit up, and he shot her a wicked grin. "I don't think you know how long I've been waiting to do this." The other Council members snickered.

Magic pulsed and snaked around him, hissing and spitting from his skin like a vicious beast. "Hmmm. Should I kill you first or make you watch while I kill your friend?"

Joan's gaze darted to Opal.

"Your friend it is."

He lobbed a knife-like magic at Opal. She was frozen, watching the magic hurtle toward her. There was nowhere to run, no way to dodge.

She closed her eyes, preparing to be skewered by the cruel man's magic.

"No!" Joan shouted, jumping in front of Opal as she opened her eyes.

The magic hit Joan, striking her through the chest. Her sword glowed as a large burst of magic ripped through the metal cage. It struck Joan's brother in the head so fast that he died with his eyes still wide open in shock.

Opal ran to Joan's side, but the sword hadn't activated

quickly enough to save her. She had collapsed to the floor. Her eyes were growing glassy, and she rasped out a breathy, "I'm sorry," before she stopped moving.

Joan's eyes still held glints of her determination into death. *She used the last of her magic and sacrificed her life to save mine. Her own people turned on her. They'll pay for their treachery.*

Red encroached Opal's vision, but this time instead of blocking it out, she embraced it. Anger threatened to overcome her. If evil would make these people pay, then she would become evil.

With the cage destroyed, her sword's magic returned in full force. As she reached for it, it glowed crimson. That was what it would take to make things even. They would need to pay in blood.

Opal kissed Joan's forehead. "Goodbye," Opal whispered. Joan's skin was as cold as ice, and the sensation made Opal's blood boil.

"You've betrayed your leader. You killed her, and many of my people, all in a futile effort to gain this sword." She grabbed the sword from Joan's unmoving body, and it glowed in her grasp. "You wanted a war? Now, you're going to get one for the history books."

The malachite on the sword's sheath cracked in two.

Excalibur vibrated in her hand. Her own sword pulsed in response. The swords pulled toward each other like opposite ends of a magnet.

Her eyes widened as the swords became one, fusing together in a swirl of gold-and-silver magic.

Opal's lips curved up in a wicked grin as she gripped the sword from the air. The hilt held a Tiger's Eye and a Fire Opal, and irresistible magic pulsed from its surface when she touched it. She slashed the sword in the Council members' direction. A burst of magic sprang out, engulfing them in a wave of gold and silver. They were burnt up by the swords' magic—her magic.

The red in her vision became brighter, and she welcomed it. She would kill all of them for this, and she would kill Amy too for ruining their chance at peace.

Opal turned her back on the carnage that she'd caused. Her dragon materialized beside her and burned down the locked door. She reached up to stroke her dragon along its neck. *I knew you'd come around.* The dragon's voice lilted, and Opal's lip quirked up in a wicked grin.

You're right, now let's test out my new power on the sorceresses' army.

AUTHOR'S NOTE

Thank you so much for reading this story. If you'd like more stories like this don't forget to leave a review. You can review "War of the Twin Swords" on Goodreads, Amazon, and Bookbub.

You can also connect with me on the following social media sites to find out about fun competitions, giveaways, and writing and self-publishing tips:

Twitter- @ButterflysDust

Instagram- @Jgghost13

Youtube- Wanderingteacherbooks

Facebook- Wanderingteacherbooks

Happy reading!

ACKNOWLEDGMENTS

Thank you to my brother for helping me polish this story and for giving me honest feedback even when I didn't want to hear it. I want to give a special thanks to my ARC and beta-reading teams for helping me take this story from good to great. Thank you to my awesome sensitivity readers for your help with Cat's character.

My mother deserves an extra special thank you. She's my biggest cheerleader and supporter and has kept me from giving up on multiple occasions. Finally, thank you to the wonderfully supportive people in the writing community and for everyone who has read this story. Your support allows me to do what I love, writing. You're all amazing, and I hope you'll read and enjoy the next book in this series, *Amy's Rebellion*.

Editors- Jami Nord, Willow Oak Author Services, Lori Diederich

Proofreader- Indie Books Gone Wild

Cover Artist- Vicki Adrian

www.ingramcontent.com/pod-product-compliance
Lightning Source LLC
Chambersburg PA
CBHW021206110726
47900CB00002B/757